*Enid Blyton's*

# The Night The Toys Had A Party

A Templar Book

Produced by Templar Publishing Company Ltd,
Pippbrook Mill, London Road, Dorking, Surrey RH4 1JE

First Published as Teddy Bear's Party by The Brockhampton Press Ltd 1945.
This edition published 1989 by Gallery Books, an imprint of W.H. Smith
Publishers, Inc., 112 Madison Avenue, New York, New York 10016. Reprinted
1990. Gallery Books are available for bulk purchase for sales promotion and
premium use. For details write or telephone the Manager of Special Sales,
W. H. Smith Publishers, Inc., 112 Madison Avenue, New York, New York 10016.
(212) 532-6600.

Text copyright © 1945 Enid Blyton.
Illustrations and design copyright © 1989 by Templar Publishing Co. Ltd.

Enid Blyton is a registered trademark of Darrell Waters Limited.

**ISBN 0 8317 6397 3**

Printed and bound by L.E.G.O., Vicenza, Italy.

# Enid Blyton's
# The Night The Toys Had A Party

## Illustrated by Sue Pearson

GALLERY BOOKS
An Imprint of W. H. Smith Publishers Inc.
112 Madison Avenue
New York City 10016

Once there was a brown teddy bear called Ben.
For a long time he lived on a shelf in a toy-shop.

Then one day a little girl bought him. She took him
home and showed him to all the toys in her nursery.

"Look!" she said. "Here is a new friend for you, toys
– a bear called Ben. Isn't he lovely! He's soft to cuddle –
and just listen to the noise he makes when I press his
middle."

"Ooooomph!" said Ben the Brown Bear, when
Sarah pressed him hard in the middle. He felt very proud
when Sarah spoke of him like that.

Sarah loved her new bear. She took him to bed with her at night, and the rag doll didn't like that, because she had always been the one to go to bed with Sarah.

Ben was proud of his growl. But the toys got very tired of it. "Ooooomph! Ooooomph! Ooooomph!" They heard the noise all night long when they got up to play.

"Stop making that noise," said the rag doll. "I'm tired of it. Go and climb back into Sarah's bed. You oughtn't to leave her if she takes you to bed at night."

"I like playing with all of you," said Ben, and he pressed his middle again. "Ooooomph! I don't leave Sarah until she's asleep, and I always go back before the morning. Ooooomph!"

Sarah gave Ben a blue ribbon to tie around his neck. He was very pleased. He stood in front of a mirror and looked at himself.

"I am a very good-looking bear, aren't I?" he said to the pink cat. She had been cleaning her fur, and she thought the bear was silly and vain. Everyone knew that the pink cat was the prettiest of all the toys. Ben thought too much of himself!

"I don't think you're at all good-looking," said the pink cat. "Your nose is too stubby, you're too fat, and I am tired of your ooooomphing."

"You're horrible," said the bear, and turned his back on the cat.

He walked away and stepped on the tail of the wind-up mouse.

"Oh – you've hurt my tail!" said the little mouse. "Say you're sorry."

"I won't!" said Ben, and he didn't.

"You haven't any manners,"
said the wind-up mouse.
"I shall go and tell the rag doll about you."
"Tattle-tale!" said Ben, and he stepped on the
mouse's tail again. The mouse squealed and tried to run
over to the rag doll to tell her about Ben. But he couldn't
because Ben wouldn't get off his tail.

Nobody felt very pleased with the bear after that.
They wouldn't play tag or hide-and-seek with him. They
wouldn't help him to untie his blue ribbon when it got into
a knot.

Ben felt very sad. He went to the oldest toy in the nursery, the wise old rocking-horse, whose long tail had once been chewed by Sarah's dog. It looked very sad. But Rocking-horse was very clever, and toys always went to him when they were in trouble.

"Rocking-horse, the toys are horrid to me," said Ben. "It makes me sad."

"Perhaps you've been nasty to them?" said Rocking-horse, swinging his chewed tail.

"I'm not – not really, anyway," said Ben. "I'd like to be nice to them, really I would. But they tell me I am horrid, and they won't let me play with them."

"Well, you be very, very nice to them and see what happens," said Rocking-horse. "Now, listen to me – you've got a birthday coming soon, haven't you?"

"Yes," said Ben. "So I have. I'd quite forgotten it!"

"Well, now, you give a lovely party for the toys," said Rocking-horse. "Give them a lovely meal, and plan lots of

games, and you'll soon see they will forget you were ever nasty."

"That's a very good idea," said Ben. "I *will* give a party! I'll think about it hard." So he did. But he wasn't used to giving parties, and he wondered how to do it.

"I must look in my piggy bank and see if I have any money there," he said to himself. "If I have, I can buy some cakes and candy and lemonade."

But there wasn't anything in his piggy bank at all, which wasn't surprising, because Ben had never put anything into it. He was sad.

"Now what shall I do?" he thought. "I really must have a party. I know! I will creep into the toy candy store when nobody is looking, and take some little bags of candy. They will do nicely for the party." Now this was very naughty of him, because it was not his candy to take. But he didn't think of that. He only thought of his party.

One night, when the toys had all gone into the toy-cupboard to have a rest after a game of hide-and-seek, Ben crept over to the toy candy store. It was a lovely place. There were tiny jars of candy, very small bars of chocolate, some little scales for weighing, and lots of paper bags to put the candy in.

"I'll take a bag of taffy," thought Ben, and he emptied some candy out of one of the jars into a bag. Then he took down another jar. It was full of tiny round chocolates. Ben tasted one to see if it was good.

Then he got a dreadful shock! Someone popped up from behind the little counter and caught him by the shoulder!

"You bad bear! You're stealing my candy!" cried an angry voice.

Ben saw that the little candy store doll was glaring at him, looking very cross.

"I wasn't stealing them! They were for my party! Everyone was going to have some," said Ben.

But the candy store doll wouldn't believe him. He called to the other toys. "Come and see this bad bear. I caught him stealing candy, and eating it, too! And all he says is that he was taking them for a party!"

"Party? What party? We've not heard of any party!" cried the toys.

Ben threw down the bags of
candy and went away with tears
in his little button eyes.
Nobody believed him.
They thought he was a bad bear.
What a pity! If only he could
have a lovely party and make
everyone happy,
the toys would be
nice to him again.

"I wonder if there are any cup cakes in the dolls' kitchen," he thought, later on. "I am sure I smelt something cooking earlier. I expect the dolls had a baking day, and baked some cup cakes in their little stove. I might ask them for some and put them away for my party."

So he went over to ask them. But when he arrived, the kitchen was empty. The dolls were all out paying a visit to the rocking-horse. Ben pushed open the door and went in. He called out softly.

"Is anybody here?" But nobody answered, because there was nobody there.

Ben went into the little kitchen. It was a lovely kitchen. The shelves were full of shiny pots and pans.

He opened the cabinet at the back of the kitchen – and there he saw a whole plate of tiny cup cakes, freshly baked!

"Good!" said Ben. "I will have these for my party.

I will tell the dolls when I see them. I am sure
they will let me have them for my party."
    He was just leaving with the plate full of
cup cakes when three of the dolls came back
from visiting the rocking-horse.

When they saw Ben coming out with their plate of cakes they were very, very cross indeed.

"Look at this naughty teddy bear!" they cried. "First he tried to take the candy and now he takes our cup cakes!" And they scolded him very severely and wouldn't listen to a word he said. None of the toys would speak to him after that, and he was very unhappy.

"I tried to do my best to have a party, but it's no good, the toys are even more unfriendly than ever!" he told the rocking-horse. "I shall run away."

"No, don't do that," said the rocking-horse. "It is a great mistake to run away from things. You set about having your party in the wrong way, you know. You should have asked the others to help you."

"I won't ask a single one of them to help me, ever!" said the bear, and he looked so angry that the rocking-horse knew it was no good talking to him any more.

The other toys came to the rocking-horse, too, and told him about the bear.

"We don't know why he is so unfriendly," they said. "He looks like a friendly bear. But he behaves so badly."

"He's a very young bear," said Rocking-horse. "He does things the wrong way. He wanted to be nice to you, really. What about being nice to him?"

"Oh, no. He doesn't deserve it," said Rag Doll.

"But it would be worth it if it makes him nice and friendly again," said Rocking-horse. "It is bad to make yourselves into enemies when you could be friends."

"Well – how could we be nice to him?" said the pink cat.

"It's his birthday next week," said Rocking-horse. "What about giving him a party? He would love that and so would you."

Now, somehow, that seemed a very good idea to the toys. They loved a party and, after all, if it was Ben the Brown Bear's birthday, he ought to have a party.

"We'll give him one," said the rag doll. "Yes, we really will!" So all the toys began to plan a fine party. But they thought they wouldn't tell the bear. It was to be a birthday surprise for him.

They went into corners and talked about it. They were always whispering together. Ben couldn't figure out what their secret was.

"They are saying horrible things about me!" he thought. "I'll run away. Yes, I really will, I won't stay in this nasty nursery."

But the toys were only planning his party. The candy store doll said he would give twelve each of his little candies and chocolates for the party.

"Oh, good!" said the pink cat. "That will be lovely. We all like your candy."

"And we will bake some cup cakes," said the dolls.

"We will make a big birthday cake, too, with two candles on it. And we will make some jam-tarts. You all like those."

"I'll make some lemonade," said the rag doll.

"Hurray!" said the wind-up mouse, "that's my favorite".

"We won't make the cup cakes or jam-tarts until the day of the birthday," said the dolls. "They will be nice and fresh then."

"We'd better give the bear some presents," said the wind-up mouse. "I could give him that blue button I found on the floor the other day."

"And I could give him my red ball," said the pink cat. "I like it very much; so I expect Ben would like it, too."

"Oh, he would," said the rag doll. "It would be a lovely present. I think I'll make him some striped pants from that material I've been saving for something special."

"Ben would look lovely in pants," said the curly-haired doll. "I'll give him a bright sash to go around his waist, to keep his pants up."

Wind-up Clown couldn't think
of anything at all to give him.
"I know," he said, "I'll paint him
a most beautiful birthday card."
"He must have a
birthday card. Everybody
does on a birthday."

Now, with all these exciting secrets going on, Ben grew more and more puzzled and sad.

Why wouldn't anyone tell him the secrets? Even Rocking-horse said nothing about them. Ben went into a corner and thought hard.

"Perhaps I am a horrid little bear," he said to himself. "I expect I am vain. And I shouldn't have gone about pressing my middle and growling all the time. I won't ooooomph any more. And – oh, dear – I shouldn't have taken the candy and cup cakes without asking!"

The more he thought about things, the worse he felt. At last he made up his mind that he was so horrid he really should go away.

He felt sure nobody in the nursery would like him any more.

"I'll creep away on my birthday," he thought. "I won't tell anybody I am going. I'll put on my hat and go."

Well, when his birthday came, there was great excitement in the nursery, because all the toys were getting ready for the party!

Little tables and chairs were set out everywhere, and cups and plates and dishes were put on them.

A delicious smell came from the dolls' kitchen, because lots of cup cakes and jam-tarts had been made – and a most beautiful birthday cake with two candles on it!

The lemonade was in a big pitcher. Little dishes of candy were on the table. The toys were dressing up in fancy clothes and getting more and more excited.

"They're having a party, and they didn't tell me anything about it," thought the bear sadly, and he went and got his hat. "I'll go now, while they are getting ready for it."

Now, just as he was walking out of the door the wind-up clown called to him.

"Hey, Ben! Where are you going?" he said.

"I'm running away. I'm a horrid little bear, and nobody here will ever like me," said Ben. "But I am sorry I was horrid. Good-bye, Wind-up Clown."

"Wait! Wait!" cried Wind-up Clown, and he ran over to Ben with the birthday card he had painted for him. "Many happy returns of the day, Ben! Here's a birthday card for you!"

"Oh – how nice of you!" said Ben, and he looked at the lovely card. "Thank you. Well, good-bye. I hope you enjoy your party."

The other toys came running up, all looking very smart. "Ben! it's *your* party, silly! It's for you. Many happy returns of the day, and please come to your own birthday party!"

Well! Ben could hardly believe his ears. His very own birthday party!

"I don't understand," he said. "How can it be mine?"

"It was a secret! We planned it for you!" said the pink cat. "Here's my present for you – a red ball to play with."

"Oh, thank you! How lovely!" said the bear. He began to feel tremendously happy. "I do wish I'd got some party clothes on, too. You all look so nice."

"Well, put some on," said the rag doll, and gave him the new striped pants. "These are for you."

"And you can tie this around your waist," said the curly-haired doll, and gave him the lovely sash.

Ben put on the striped pants and the sash. They did look handsome.

The wind-up mouse gave him the blue button he had found, and the curly-haired doll sewed it on the front of his pants. Ben looked at himself in the mirror. He thought he looked very handsome indeed – but he didn't say so! He let the others say it for him!

"You look fine, Ben! You look wonderful!" they cried. "The pants fit you well."

"And now let's have the party," said Rocking-horse as the dolls came out carrying plates of cookies and tarts – and a big plate with the birthday cake on it!

"Many happy returns of the day!" they cried, and Ben felt happier than ever. How nice everyone was! How could he ever have thought they were horrid?

They sat down to the party. The cookies were delicious. The jam-tarts were lovely. The candy was the nicest Ben had ever eaten. The lemonade was very tasty.

All the toys drank to Ben's health. Then they cut the birthday cake. Ben had to cut the first slice, because it was his birthday. After that the wind-up clown helped him, because there were so many slices to cut.

"Wish when you take the first bite!" cried the curly-haired doll. "You always have to do that with birthday cakes!"

So everyone wished.

Then the toys cleared away the party things, the chairs and tables were set aside, and the party games began. They played hide-and-seek and pin-the-tail-on-the-donkey, and then a lively game of musical chairs.

Everyone was happy and sleepy when the party was over. They climbed into the toy-cupboard to go to sleep – all except Ben, who crept, as usual, into Sarah's bed!

"Where have you been, Ben?" said Sarah, waking up.

"Oooomph!" said Ben, sleepily. "To my birthday party. I've had a lovely time. And I do think the toys are the very nicest in all the world. I shall never, never run away from them!"

"Your *birthday party!*" said Sarah. "I must be asleep and dreaming!" But she knew she hadn't been asleep when, next morning, she saw Ben the Brown Bear still dressed in his party clothes! It was quite true, wasn't it? He *had* been to his party – and what a lovely one it was!